BEAR IN A BOAT IN THE BORD___.

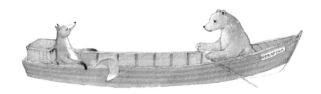

Published in Great Britain
by SERAFINA PRESS
The Smokehouse Gallery
St Ella's Place
Eyemouth
Berwickshire
TD14 5HP
www.serafinapress.co.uk

ISBN 0-9552696-3-6
ISBN 978-0-9552696-3-9

First published in Great Britain in 2008

Printed in Great Britain by Martins the Printers, Berwick upon Tweed
www.martins-the-printers.com

BEAR IN A BOAT IN THE BORDERS

Cara Lockhart Smith & Jennifer T. Doherty

Illustrated by Cara Lockhart Smith

SERAFINA PRESS

For Laura Doherty and Gerry Morgan, pirate kings, both.
With love.
J.T.D.

For the Byfields of Huddersfield,
Matty, Jo and Reuben,
&
for the Wilsons of Bognor Regis,
Tony and Sue.
C.L.S.

Where the lonely moorland stream becomes a shining river,
a Bear got into his boat. He rowed and he rowed....

.... till he came to a tower on a hill. Down by the waterside, a fox sat in the sun.

"Hello, Bear, where are you going?"

"I'm off to the Fair in Berwick Town."

"I want to go to that Fair myself," said the fox.

"Well then, do," said the Bear.

So the fox jumped into the boat, and they carried on down the river.

They came to a town where crowds were celebrating on the green beside the water. "Oh, I do love to dance!" said the fox.

He jumped out of the boat and joined the revels. The Bear in the boat waited patiently by the bank.

At last the fox returned
with a griffin and an ape.

"Ahoy!" said the ape.
"Humph!" said the griffin.
"My friends are travelling with us
to Berwick Town," said the fox.
  So they all jumped into the boat, and
the Bear rowed on down the river.

They came to a great house set by the water. There, on the bank, an old man and his dog were walking by the river.

"Oh, I do love to stroll in the sunshine!" said the fox, and he jumped on to the bank and sauntered up and down.

When the fox returned to the boat, the dog was with him.

"My pal the dog is coming too," said the fox.

The Bear sighed but said nothing.

"Goodbye," waved the man. "Be home before dawn."

The Bear rowed on down the river. They floated past ruins, and under bridges. On and on they went, through the sunlit countryside.

At last they came to a
great pale castle. There
in the meadow was a
leaping hare. "Oh I do
love a hop, skip and
jump!" said the fox, and
he leapt out of the boat....

.... and cavorted about with the hare.

The fox came back leading the hare by one ear. "My friend the hare just has to come to the Fair!" said the fox.

So the hare jumped into the boat. It wobbled a little and the Bear looked worried, but he still rowed on. As they floated towards the bridge with the marriage house built in its side, they saw an otter swimming beside the boat.

"Oh, I do love a splish-splash, me!" said the fox, and he dived right in.

"Shove up for my buddy the otter!" said the fox, as he clambered back into the boat.

By now the boat was so laden it was low down on the water. The Bear was exhausted. "Keep rowing, my friend, it's not far now," said the fox.

Then just as they were passing a house in a wood on a hill, a seagull flew off from a rock and headed for the boat.

"Full up!" said the fox. But the seagull kept on coming. It landed....

.... on the head of the fox. The fox....

.... swatted at the seagull but hit the ape.

The ape jumped up and jostled the griffin, who....

.... picked up his carpet bag and twirled it at the ape....

.... but hit the dog. The dog snapped at the griffin but....

.... frightened the hare. The hare leapt up and barged....

.... the otter. The otter slithered sideways....

.... and clawed the bear on his nose.

"OW!"

said the Bear.

It was too much altogether. The boat turned topsy-turvy, and everyone fell in the water.

Then the Bear climbed back into the boat, and picked up the oars.
"I've had enough of these shenanigans. Find your own way to the Fair," he growled.

So the hare lolloped along the river path, and the fox sauntered arm-in-arm
with the griffin and the ape, and the seagull flew....

.... and the dog doggy-paddled, and the
otter swam underwater....

.... and all in their own good time they got to Berwick Town, which was just round the bend.

There, on the grassy land by the waterside, was the entrance to the Fair.

Music was playing. The carousels went round and round.

So the Bear and the fox and the griffin and the ape and the hare and the dog and the otter, and even the seagull, all enjoyed the Fun of the Fair.

At the end of the evening, they gave the prizes they had won to the patient Bear, as a thank-you for rowing them to the Fair in Berwick Town.

Even the fox gave him a stray balloon.

Round about midnight they all got back in the boat.

Then quietly, slowly, sleepily, happily, the Bear
rowed them back up-river to their homes.